BIGGEST NAMES IN SPORTS

CHRISTIAN YELICH

BASEBALL STAR

by Lee Patrick

FOCUS READERS

NAVIGATOR

WWW.FOCUSREADERS.COM

Focus Readers is distributed by North Star Editions:
sales@northstareditions.com | 888-417-0195

Produced for Focus Readers by Red Line Editorial.

Photographs ©: Lawrence Iles/Icon Sportswire/AP Images, cover, 1; Larry Radloff/Icon Sportswire, 4–5, 7, 9; Tom DiPace/AP Images, 10–11; Tom Priddy/Four Seam Images/AP Images, 13; Cliff Welch/Icon Sportswire, 15; Chris Schneider/AP Images, 16–17; Juan Salas/Icon Sportswire, 18; Warren Wimmer/Icon Sportswire, 21; Lawrence Iles/Icon Sportswire, 22–23; Matt Marton/AP Images, 25; Gene J. Puskar/AP Images, 27; Red Line Editorial, 29

Library of Congress Cataloging-in-Publication Data
Library of Congress Cataloging-in-Publication Data is available on the Library of Congress website.

ISBN
978-1-64493-057-1 (hardcover)
978-1-64493-136-3 (paperback)
978-1-64493-294-0 (ebook pdf)
978-1-64493-215-5 (hosted ebook)

Printed in the United States of America
Mankato, MN
012020

ABOUT THE AUTHOR

Lee Patrick is a children's book editor and writer based in the Upper Peninsula of Michigan. He has worked on books covering a variety of subjects. He enjoys cross-country skiing and ice fishing. He lives with his wife and golden retriever, Hamilton.

TABLE OF CONTENTS

POSTSEASON
22

CHAPTER 1

COMING UP BIG

The pitch sped through the air toward home plate. Christian Yelich was ready for it. The Milwaukee Brewers slugger swung his bat hard. The ball flew high into the air and soared into deep left-center field. The outfielders could only watch as the ball sailed over the fence for a two-run homer.

Yelich prepares for a pitch during a 2018 playoff game against the Colorado Rockies.

Brewers fans cheered loudly as Yelich rounded the bases.

Yelich was playing in his first playoff game with the Brewers. Milwaukee was facing the Colorado Rockies in the first round of the 2018 National League (NL) playoffs. Yelich's third-inning home run put the Brewers ahead 2–0 in Game 1 of the series.

In the sixth inning, Yelich stepped into the batter's box once again. This time he lined the ball up the middle of the infield. Yelich sprinted toward first base. Meanwhile, the second baseman gathered the ball and threw it to first. But Yelich was too quick. He reached base safely on

Yelich cranks out a home run against the Rockies.

an infield single. It was Yelich's second hit of the game.

By the end of the ninth inning, the game was tied 2–2. In the 10th inning, Yelich stood at the plate with two strikes.

He waited patiently for a good pitch. When none came, he reached first base on a walk. If Yelich could score, Milwaukee would win the game.

Yelich advanced to second base on a wild pitch. Then he ran to third on a groundout. Brewers third baseman Mike

ANOTHER BIG PERFORMANCE

At the end of the 2018 season, the Brewers and Chicago Cubs were tied for first place in the NL Central Division. The teams faced off in a one-game playoff to decide the division winner. Yelich played a key role in Milwaukee's offense. He went 3-for-4 with a run batted in (RBI) to help the Brewers defeat the Cubs 3–1 and win the division.

A Brewers teammate greets Yelich at the plate as he scores a run.

Moustakas stepped up to the plate. He cracked a hit into right field. Yelich trotted in easily from third to score. The Brewers had won the game.

CHAPTER 2

A QUICK RISE

Christian Yelich was born in Thousand Oaks, California, on December 5, 1991. Growing up, Christian always had an interest in baseball. But his family had more history with football. In fact, one of his great-grandparents had played in the National Football League. Even so, Christian decided to play baseball.

Yelich takes part in a minor league game in 2010.

After all, that's what most of his friends were playing.

As a kid, Christian stood out from his teammates because of how well he could hit. He also developed the skills to be

PLAYING AGAINST TOP TALENT

Christian Yelich faced tough competition in high school in Southern California. At Westlake High School, he played against a handful of future major league players. That included Nolan Arenado of the Colorado Rockies. The two matched up in high school and went on to successful major league careers. In 2018, both Yelich and Arenado finished in the top three in the vote for the NL Most Valuable Player (MVP) award.

Yelich warms up before a 2011 game with the Greensboro Grasshoppers, a minor league team.

a good outfielder. Soon, major league **scouts** became interested in Christian. They talked about **drafting** him when he graduated from high school in 2010.

After Yelich finished high school, he had the opportunity to play college baseball at the University of Miami.

However, he decided to go straight into professional baseball instead. The Florida Marlins selected Yelich in the first round of the 2010 Major League Baseball (MLB) Draft.

Yelich joined the Marlins' **farm system** right away. He impressed the coaches by hitting the ball consistently. The coaches were confident that he could hit a pitch no matter where it was. Yelich was also a good base runner. But coaches believed he still needed to work on his defense.

After a great season in 2011, Yelich earned the Marlins' minor league player of the year award. He won the award again in 2012 after another successful

Yelich runs to field a ball during a game with the minor league Jacksonville Suns in 2013.

year. Coaches and teammates talked about how hard Yelich worked. He spent hours practicing hitting and getting in the best shape possible.

The hard work paid off. In July 2013, Yelich got the call every player dreams of. He was heading to the major leagues.

CHAPTER 3

A MAJOR LEAGUE PLAYER

Christian Yelich made his major league **debut** with the Marlins in July 2013. The bright spotlight of the major leagues did not startle Yelich. In his first game, he racked up two hits. Yelich stayed with the Marlins for the rest of that season. He continued to reach base by getting hits and drawing walks.

Yelich hits a single to right field in the first game of his MLB career.

Yelich makes a play in the outfield during a 2014 game against the Atlanta Braves.

Yelich's role increased in 2014. He became the team's **leadoff hitter**. Opposing teams knew he wouldn't swing at bad pitches. So they started throwing more strikes. And that led to more hits.

Meanwhile, Yelich was improving on defense. In 2014, he mostly played left field. It was a great fit for Yelich. At the end of the season, he won the Gold Glove Award. That award is given to the league's best defensive player at each position.

By 2015, Yelich was part of an outfield filled with young stars. He played with Giancarlo Stanton and Marcell Ozuna. Fans began to get excited about how much these three could help improve the team. But it didn't go as planned.

Early in 2015, both Yelich and Ozuna struggled at the plate. That caused the Marlins to lose games and fall behind in the standings. The two players improved their hitting later in the season. But by then it was too late.

The Marlins were too far behind the other teams to reach the playoffs. The next season, the Marlins missed the playoffs once again.

After the 2017 season, former New York Yankees legend Derek Jeter became part owner of the Marlins. Jeter was now in charge of the team's operations. He

PLAYING FOR HIS COUNTRY

Yelich made a name for himself during the 2017 World Baseball Classic. The top baseball players in the world take part in this tournament. Each player competes for his home country. Yelich played for Team USA and helped the United States win the tournament for the first time ever.

Yelich rounds the bases after blasting a home run against the Chicago Cubs in 2015.

decided to trade away the Marlins' star players. He planned to rebuild the team with younger talent. The Marlins traded away Stanton in November 2017. In December, they parted with Ozuna. Then in January 2018, Miami traded Yelich to the Milwaukee Brewers.

CHAPTER 4

MEETING EXPECTATIONS

In 2018, Christian Yelich joined a talented Brewers team. Milwaukee had nearly made the playoffs the season before. Yelich had to prove himself in order to become a regular starter for the Brewers.

The right-field fence in Milwaukee is shorter than it is in Miami's home park.

Yelich swings for the fences during his first season with the Milwaukee Brewers.

And Yelich took full advantage of that fact. He became a regular starter by slugging home runs. He also hit for a high **batting average**.

Milwaukee stayed near the top of the division standings early in the 2018 season. Yelich was a big reason for the team's success. Midway through the season, he played in his first **All-Star Game**. He made an impact by hitting a key home run late in the game.

Yelich came back from the All-Star Game ready to help Milwaukee make the playoffs. But the Brewers trailed the Chicago Cubs in the standings. In the final month, Yelich was one of the best

Yelich gets a hit during a 2018 game against the Chicago Cubs, helping the Brewers win the NL Central.

hitters in the National League. He helped the Brewers win their division and qualify for the playoffs.

In the first round, Yelich's heroics helped the Brewers **sweep** the Rockies.

Then they came within a game of the 2018 World Series before falling to the Los Angeles Dodgers. Yelich earned the NL MVP award for his great 2018 season.

Yelich didn't slow down in 2019. He still got plenty of hits. But he started hitting more home runs. In the first half of the

AFTER THE FIRE

After becoming a major league player, Yelich bought a house in California. It was near where he grew up. In 2018, he had to leave his home because of wildfires. His home did not burn down, but many others did. Yelich and other professional athletes decided to help the people who lost their homes. They raised more than $1 million through events such as charity softball games.

Yelich scores a run against the Pittsburgh Pirates in 2019.

season, Yelich blasted 31 homers. That was the most in the league. Milwaukee seemed like a perfect fit for Yelich. Brewers fans hoped he could help lead the team to its first World Series title.

CHRISTIAN YELICH

- Height: 6 feet 3 inches (191 cm)
- Weight: 195 pounds (88 kg)
- Birth date: December 5, 1991
- Birthplace: Thousand Oaks, California
- High school: Westlake High School (Westlake Village, California)
- Minor league teams: GCL Marlins; Greensboro Grasshoppers; Jupiter Hammerheads; Jacksonville Suns; New Orleans Zephyrs
- MLB teams: Miami Marlins (2013–2017); Milwaukee Brewers (2018–)
- Major awards: NL MVP (2018); NL Batting Champion (2018); Gold Glove Award (2014)

Milwaukee
Greensboro
Thousand Oaks
Jacksonville
Jupiter
New Orleans
Miami

FOCUS ON
CHRISTIAN YELICH

Write your answers on a separate piece of paper.

1. Write a letter to a friend describing Yelich's first season with the Milwaukee Brewers.

2. Do you think the Marlins should have traded Yelich to the Brewers? Why or why not?

3. Which team drafted Yelich in 2010?

A. Milwaukee Brewers
B. Florida Marlins
C. Colorado Rockies

4. Why might the Marlins have traded Yelich to the Brewers?

A. Yelich had not helped the Marlins reach the playoffs.
B. The Marlins didn't think Yelich could play well in hot weather.
C. Yelich was unhappy living in Florida and wanted to move.

Answer key on page 32.

GLOSSARY

All-Star Game

A game in which the league's best players take part.

batting average

The number of hits a player has divided by the number of times at bat.

debut

First appearance.

drafting

Selecting a player in a draft. A draft is a system that allows teams to acquire new players who are coming into a league.

farm system

A group of teams that help players develop their skills. Each MLB team has its own farm system. Good players usually move up to higher levels in the system.

leadoff hitter

The player who bats first in a baseball lineup.

scouts

People whose jobs involve looking for talented young players.

sweep

Winning all the games in a series.

TO LEARN MORE

BOOKS

Braun, Eric. *Stathead Baseball: How Data Changed the Sport*. North Mankato, MN: Compass Point Books, 2019.

Fishman, Jon M. *Giancarlo Stanton*. Minneapolis: Lerner Publications, 2018.

Lyon, Drew. *A Superfan's Guide to Pro Baseball Teams*. North Mankato, MN: Capstone Press, 2018.

NOTE TO EDUCATORS

Visit **www.focusreaders.com** to find lesson plans, activities, links, and other resources related to this title.

INDEX

Answer Key: 1. Answers will vary; **2.** Answers will vary; **3.** B; **4.** A